Cat Tales

Shop Cat

Cat Tales

Shop Cat

LINDA NEWBERY

Illustrated by Stephen Lambert

USBORNE

With love to Jon, who gave me the title

First published in the UK in 2009 by Usborne Publishing Ltd.,
Usborne House, 83-85 Saffron Hill, London EC1N 8RT, England.
www.usborne.com

Text copyright © Linda Newbery, 2009

Illustration copyright © Usborne Publishing Ltd., 2009

A CIP catalogue record for this book is available from the British Library.

JFMAMJJASON /08   ISBN 9780746097304   Printed in Great Britain.

Chapter One

The cat turned up one Tuesday
lunchtime, and no one ever found out
where she came from.

There she was, curled up fast asleep in
the front window – a small, neat cat.
Hattie stopped outside to look, thinking
at first it was a toy she hadn't seen before.

A very lifelike one! Cat-sized, with real whiskers, and fur of a rich, dark colour – not black, not ginger, but a mixture of both. There she slept, on the patterned cloth Uncle Theo had spread out in the window where toys were displayed. She was snuggled between a big panda and a model lighthouse.

Hattie went inside. She came here every day after school, to help Uncle Theo until Mum collected her on the way home from work. She knew she was lucky to have a great-uncle with his own toyshop. Teddy and May, it was called. Teddy was Uncle Theo, and May was Aunty May, who'd died last year. But the shop would always be Teddy and May, because it sounded so nice.

On the shop sign, Teddy was a smart teddy bear, and May a smiling doll.

"No, I don't know whose cat she is," Uncle Theo was saying to a customer. "She just walked in."

"Cats are like that," said the man. *Ting!* went the doorbell as he left, carrying the jigsaw puzzle he'd bought.

Uncle Theo gave Hattie a kiss and a cuddle, then fetched her a glass of juice and a ginger biscuit from the back kitchen. With her mouth full, she went to the window for a closer look at the cat.

"How d'you know she's a she?" she asked her uncle.

"Tortoiseshells generally are," Uncle Theo told her. "A male would be ginger."

Tortoiseshell! Hattie liked the word –

though she'd never seen a tortoise with a
shell of such rich, glowing colour. The cat
was so still that it was hard to believe she
wasn't a toy, like the panda next to her.

11

Hattie couldn't resist reaching out to stroke the lovely fur. At once the cat stretched and yawned, showing sharp white teeth.

"You *are* real!" said Hattie.

The cat certainly was. It looked back at her, with eyes that were bright and very green. At once, Hattie saw that this was a *clever* cat. Sharpness and cleverness shone from those green, green eyes.

I know you, those eyes seemed to say. *I knew I'd find you here.*

The cat jumped down from the window, and began to twist and twine herself round Hattie's legs – round and round, between her feet, in and out. Her back was arched and her tail high. She purred loudly, as if to say, *I'll be your friend.*

"She did that before, when she first came in," said Uncle Theo. "Nearly tripped me up."

"What will you call her?"

Uncle Theo shook his head. "Oh, I shan't give her a name. She belongs to someone, I'm sure. They'll come and find her."

Hattie hoped no one would. The cat had come here to find *her*. Those sharp green eyes seemed to say so, quite clearly.

Chapter Two

Next day the tortoiseshell was still there; and the day after, and the day after that. She had the look of a cat who was here to stay.

In spite of Uncle Theo's warning, Hattie had given her a name – Twister, because of the way she twined and

twisted herself round people's legs.
Special people's legs.

Uncle Theo had put up a sign on the front door:

But so far, no one *had* asked.

Sometimes Twister curled up, fast asleep. At other times she sat up very straight, gazing out at the street with her wise green eyes. People looked in at her, exclaiming over how real she looked, how lifelike. Then Twister would give one blink and confuse them.

Hattie began to think she did it on purpose.

"*Do* you?" she asked, and Twister gave her a look that seemed to say, *Wouldn't you like to know?*

Because Uncle Theo was busy serving customers, or unpacking new toys in the storeroom, Hattie took over the job of getting Twister's dinner each evening, just before closing time. Out in the back kitchen, she'd tap a fork against a saucer, and Twister would come running, tail high.

Uncle Theo bought tins of cat food,
and cat biscuits, and cat litter, and he
made a cushion-bed in the window.
Each night he invited Twister up to his
flat above the shop, but she preferred
her window cushion.

"Likes to keep an eye on things, our shop cat," said Uncle Theo.

Hattie didn't go to Teddy and May at weekends. She and Mum went swimming, and visited Mum's friend Sarah. They fed the ducks in the park and swung on the swings.

Back at home, Hattie looked around, feeling that something was missing. It was a cosy little house, just right for Hattie and Mum, but it needed something extra.

"Mum," she said. "Couldn't Twister come and live with us?"

Mum looked surprised. "Well – I'm fond of cats. I had one when I was your age. But Uncle Theo seems to like her.

She'll probably stay with him."

"I wish she was *my* cat," said Hattie. "I think that's what she wants."

"Let's wait and see if her owner turns up," said Mum. "You might end up disappointed if you start thinking she's yours. Besides, do we really know what Twister thinks?"

Hmm, Hattie thought, *I do*!

She was glad when Monday came, and the end of school, and she rushed down the street to Teddy and May.

Twister wasn't in the front window. Hattie's heart gave a thud. But – yes! As she went in Uncle Theo pointed, and there Twister was, perching high on a shelf with the Russian dolls. She jumped down to twine herself round  Hattie's legs, then sprang up again to sit behind a train set.

"We like your shop cat," said a voice. "She's very beautiful!"

Hattie turned round. The voice belonged to a grey-haired lady who'd followed Hattie in. She wore a purple raincoat with bright yellow flowers all over it – although it wasn't raining – and a mauve squashy hat. With her was a balding man who wore a big overcoat – although it wasn't cold. They were both plump and short, with kind faces.

"She's not really my cat," said Uncle Theo. "I don't know who she belongs to."

"Cats have a way of deciding these things for themselves," said the man.

He and the grey-haired lady stayed for quite a while, looking at everything in the shop. Uncle Theo went back to the storeroom, to put price labels on a model army that had just arrived, but Hattie

stayed by the counter, wanting to be
helpful.

"Are you looking for a special present
for someone?" she asked.

"No, no," said the man. "We're just
looking. We like toys."

They didn't leave until Hattie went out to the kitchen to get Twister's dinner. When she came back into the shop with Uncle Theo, to lock up and turn the sign round to say CLOSED, the visitors had gone. She hadn't even heard the *ting!* of the doorbell.

"Hmm." Hattie was disappointed. "They didn't buy a single thing! After they spent so long looking! I thought they'd buy *loads* of toys. They looked as if they might."

"Never mind," said Uncle Theo. "Maybe they'll come back. Some people like to spend a long time choosing."

Mum sometimes said that Uncle Theo wasn't very good at shopkeeping, and Hattie thought maybe she had a point. He didn't seem to mind whether he sold anything or not. He just liked having the shop, and people coming in. If they found exactly the right toy, he was happy. But he was every bit as pleased if they looked around, said something nice, and went away.

What he *didn't* like was when children saw a toy they really wanted, but didn't have enough money. They didn't always say, but sometimes Uncle Theo saw disappointment on a child's face, and that made him sad.

There'd been a little boy, two weeks ago, who picked up a red tractor and clutched it under his arm until his mother took it from him and put it back on the shelf. "You'll have to wait till your birthday, and that's a *long* time," she told him. "There's no spare money." As she led him out of the shop, the boy turned his head for one last look at the red tractor. He didn't cry, but he looked as if he wanted to.

Hattie's mum had just come in, and was talking to Uncle Theo. Hattie saw Uncle Theo make up his mind, and move towards the shelf – but Mum guessed what he was about to do, and grabbed his arm. "They'll be back," she told him. "You can't go giving toys away! That's no way to run a business!"

Uncle Theo shook his head, and laughed at himself, because he knew she was right – but all the same he looked sadly through the window at the boy and mother as they walked away.

"Aunty May was never so soft," Mum scolded. "Really – I wonder what you get up to, when you're here on your own! You need an assistant, to keep an eye on you."

"I've got one! Hattie," said Uncle Theo proudly. "She's a big help."

Now that Twister was here, Uncle Theo had a new helper. Twister was clever: Hattie had seen that at once. But she didn't realize just *how* clever.

Chapter Three

Now that she felt at home, Twister found various sitting places. In the fireplace, where the rag dolls lived. On the table in the middle, which had enough animals to fill a zoo, or at least a fairly large ark. She'd lie down and sleep with the sausage-snakes, or play with the marbles, or chase the clockwork soldiers. One afternoon she squashed herself inside the dolls' house.

It took Hattie a long time to put all the tables and chairs and the tiny cups and saucers back in their places.

But the funny thing was that Twister often showed the customers just the thing they wanted to buy.

"Ooh look, marbles!
Real old-
fashioned
marbles!" said
an aunty, when
Twister had
swiped one
across the floor. "You don't see those
very often! I'm going to get a whole bag."

Or:

"Just look at this
cat, sitting on
a crocodile!"
exclaimed a dad.

"Would you like that, Zak, for your birthday? It's got such a lovely smiley face." And when they left the shop, Zak was happily cuddling a crocodile that was much bigger than he was.

Or:

"Train station! Train station! With a cat – a real cat!"

When Uncle Theo sold a clown made of springs, a dog on wheels, and an astronaut, all within half an hour, he and Hattie began to watch Twister very carefully.

"How do you do it, Twister?" Hattie asked. The cat gave a cool green stare, blinked once, and began to wash her paws.

"Those two people came in again today," Uncle Theo told Hattie. "Yesterday as well, only I forgot to tell you. The lady in the flowery mac, and the man with the shiny head."

"Good!" said Hattie. "What did they buy?"

"Oh, they didn't buy anything. They spent a long time looking, chatted a bit, then went away."

Hattie thought hard about this while she put out a model windmill and three wooden giraffes. There was something odd about that man and lady.

She thought about the lady's mac and the man's thick overcoat – strange clothes to be wearing in summer, when it wasn't cold or raining. Was it because those coats had big pockets – big *deep* pockets?

Hattie hesitated, thinking about what Mum said about Uncle Theo. That he was too kind, too good-natured. Too willing to see good in everyone. What if—

"What if they're *not* just looking round?" She had to say it. "What if they're – you know – taking things?"

"Shoplifters?" Uncle Theo looked severely shocked. "Oh, no. Surely not. They don't *look* like thieves."

"What *do* thieves look like?"

"Well, I don't really know," said Uncle Theo. "But not like that. Anyway, nothing's gone missing!"

Hmm, Hattie thought. But would he know if it *had*?

She liked Uncle Theo just as he was – he wouldn't be Uncle Theo if he was all scowly and suspicious. But Mum's point was that a shopkeeper needed to keep his eyes open, in case a customer tried to sneak out without paying, or slipped a small toy into a bag when they thought he wasn't looking. Aunty May had been much sharper, much beadier-eyed. She'd been in charge of the money, while Uncle Theo ordered the toys, and unpacked them when they arrived, and arranged them on the shelves. If something had gone missing, Aunty May would have known at once.

Hattie thought again about those big coats, and those big pockets. She was going to watch that lady and man very carefully indeed, next time they came in. She'd be Uncle Theo's sharp lookout, whenever she was in the shop.

"You'll keep an eye on things, won't you?" she asked Twister. And Twister gave her a look that seemed to say, *Two eyes*.

That cat, Hattie felt sure, knew exactly what was going on.

Chapter Four

While Hattie was thinking her
suspicious thoughts, a girl was looking
round the shop. Hattie tried to smile at
her, but the girl didn't look her way. She
spent ages deciding – picking things up,
looking at them longingly, then putting
them back. After two or three tours of

the shelves, she went to where Twister was sitting, near the small carved animals. At last she approached Uncle Theo at the counter.

"Er – there's no price on this. How much is it? I prob'ly haven't got enough, but—" Her voice trailed away.

What she'd chosen was a wooden box, a little painted one. Hattie had never seen it before, so went over to look. It had a pattern of ducks and reeds against blue water and blue sky.

Uncle Theo picked it up and looked at it. His eyebrows shot up like arrows.
"Where did you find this?"

"Over there." The girl pointed to where Twister sat watching, high on the shelf. "It's for my little brother's birthday." Her voice was quiet enough to slither through the floorboards. "He *loves* ducks. But I haven't got much."

She was unzipping a small purse, looking in. The coins inside made only the feeblest clink.

Uncle Theo turned the little box over and over in his hands. He opened the hinged lid, revealing a green satin lining, and a small china duck.

"Beautiful," he muttered. "Handmade, must be. But how did it get here?" Then he looked at the girl's anxious face, and handed her the box. "You can have it. For your brother. I hope he'll be pleased."

"But – how much?" said the girl.

"Nothing." Uncle Theo brushed the question away. "It's yours. Erm – a special offer. If you buy one of these gift tags – see, only forty pence – you get a free box to go with it."

"What—" The girl's eyes had gone big and round. "But—"

And Uncle Theo had to do a lot more persuading before she actually believed that she could have the duck box for only forty pence. She counted out coins, then thanked him nine times before she left.

Uncle Theo smiled and waved as she turned to look back through the window, and so did Hattie. Then Hattie gave him a stern look.

"You know what Mum would say! That's no way to run a business. Giving things away!"

"But it's made that girl happy," said Uncle Theo, still smiling. "And it'll make her brother happy. And that makes *me* happy. What could be better than that? Besides, I don't remember buying that box in the first place. It'd be wrong to take money for it."

"So where *did* it come from?"

"I don't know. I can only think that it's been here for ages and ages, so long I've forgotten," said Uncle Theo.

"Maybe it got pushed to the back of the shelf."

"Hmm," went Hattie. This explanation was too ordinary to be true. What if someone had left it here by mistake, and came back specially, only to find it gone? Uncle Theo hadn't thought about this carefully enough, it seemed to her.

She gave Twister a frowny look. "Do you know anything about this?"

Twister's stare seemed to say, *I might. I might not.* And she began washing her paws.

But the duck box was only the start.

Chapter Five

Next Monday, when Hattie arrived at
Teddy and May, Uncle Theo reported
that a little boy had come up to the
counter with another unpriced box –
this time with a pattern of teddy bears
on it, and a carved wooden bear inside.

"Hmm. And where was Twister at the

time?" Hattie asked.

Uncle Theo looked vague. "Oh, somewhere around. Can't remember."

"So, let me guess," said Hattie. "You gave away the box for nothing?"

"Of course! Now, I know you'll say, *That's no way to make money*. But you'd be wrong! The boy's dad bought a clown and a digger as well. Then there was the other one."

"The other what?"

"The other box. With daisies on it, and a blue lining – *very* nice. A little girl found that for her twin sister, on Saturday morning. Then she bought a set of dominoes, and her mum bought a pirate. So, you see, takings have been quite good."

Twister had jumped down from the window to weave around Hattie's legs. Hattie looked round the whole shop for more mysterious boxes, but couldn't find a single one. She had the silliest idea that Twister might somehow be *making* them – but how could a cat make a wooden box? And paint it so nicely? Or make a cushiony satin lining?

Maybe Twister magicked them out of the air? But that was just crazy. Twister was a special cat – but a *magical* cat? That was something else.

She looked at Twister, who was now sitting neatly next to a space rocket, and Twister gave her a green stare in return.

Just then the doorbell jangled, and in came the man in the overcoat and the lady in the flowery mac. They both smiled at Hattie, who was looking after the counter while Uncle Theo was busy in the storeroom. The lady wore red shoes with bows and pointy toes, and a different hat – a green one with a red poppy stuck in it.

"Hello, dear," she said, as if she was Hattie's nan.

"Good afternoon," Hattie answered, in her best – and rather suspicious – Shop Voice. "Can I help you?"

"Oh, that's all right, dear," said the lady. "We're just looking." And together they shuffled along to look at the patchwork turtles.

It was *very* hot outside today; no one else wore a coat. *Hmm*, thought Hattie. She pretended to tidy up the beads and dice on the counter, but really she was watching the strange pair, following their every move. There! Yes! The man

was rummaging in his pockets; then
they both looked round to see if anyone
was looking, and the woman delved in
hers. Very deep pockets, their coats
seemed to have.

Shoplifters! Definitely! If anyone had

ever lifted a shop, it was these two.

Hattie's head was buzzing with excitement. When Uncle Theo came back, she nudged him, and whispered in his ear: "They *are*! Shoplifters, like I said! They're doing it now!"

Uncle Theo looked most upset. "Oh dear," he muttered. "I wish they wouldn't. I suppose I'd better say something."

"Course you should!" hissed Hattie. "You can't let them get *away* with it."

"Wait, though," mumbled Uncle Theo. "They might be going to pay."

But they weren't. They moved slowly towards the door, admiring all the toys they passed on the way, and then the man called out brightly, "Bye-bye! See you again soon!" and they were out in the street.

54

"Come on!" Hattie wasn't going to let Uncle Theo stand and think what to do next. She pulled at his sleeve, dragging him through the door and out. She wouldn't have been surprised if the pair of thieves had sprinted away fast, in spite of the weight of their pockets, but instead they were standing outside looking pleased. The lady was saying, "How about a nice cup of tea?"

Hattie pulled Uncle Theo up to them. "Go *on*!"

Uncle Theo cleared his throat. "Erm. I think. Maybe. I wonder if you'd accompany me back inside? Hattie here thinks you've been...acting suspiciously."

At once, the lady burst into noisy tears. She pulled a flowery handkerchief out of her pocket, and dabbed her eyes.

"Oh, Basil!" she wailed. "I *knew* we wouldn't get away with it! I *knew* we'd get caught!"

An admission of guilt! Hattie stood with her arms folded, very stern. What next? Should Uncle Theo call the police?

"Now, Rosemary, don't get upset," said the man. "We can explain."

"So you *were* shoplifting?" said Uncle Theo.

The man, Basil, drew himself up to his full height, though he wasn't very tall. "Shop*lifting*? Excuse *me*. No, no. We're not shop*lifters*—"

"We're shop-*givers*," snuffled Rosemary. "Haven't you seen our lovely boxes?"

There was a pause. Then Uncle Theo said, "Oh dear, dear. Those are *your* boxes? I'm afraid I've been giving them away."

"Wait a minute!" Hattie wanted to get this clear. "Shop-*givers*? You give things to shops?"

"Only to *this* shop—" said the man, and, "I know it sounds silly—" began the woman.

Uncle Theo held up his hand. "Let's go back inside, and talk about this over a cup of tea."

Everyone looked relieved. Rosemary stopped crying, and even began to smile.

They all sat on the squashy cushions in the corner. Uncle Theo brought tea and carrot cake, with orange juice for

Hattie. Twister sat next to her, on the dragon rug.

"You see," Rosemary explained, "we're very fond of children, but we haven't any of our own. We haven't even got grandchildren. Not a single nephew or niece."

"But we like toys, and we like children, and we love toyshops," said Basil. "So it's a shame we haven't any children to give our boxes to. We make them between us – she does the woodwork, you know, and I do the painting and varnishing. And of course we want children to have them."

"So," said Rosemary, "we were delighted when we discovered Teddy and May. The perfect place to leave our

boxes for children to find! I'm sorry if we've been sneaky."

"No, no, no. No problem at all," said Uncle Theo. "That seems sensible enough to me."

"But," Hattie put in, "why doesn't Uncle Theo *pay* you for the boxes, then sell them?"

"Yes, I could do that," Uncle Theo agreed.

Basil looked shocked. "Oh, no. We couldn't take *money*. It wouldn't be the same."

"If you don't mind," said Rosemary, "we'll just carry on as we are."

Hmm, thought Hattie. *Someone* here needed to be businesslike.

"What you should do," she told Uncle

Theo, "is place orders. Say, ten duck boxes. Ten with teddies. Ten with flowers. You know people like them."

Uncle Theo stirred his tea very thoughtfully; then laughed. "Shall we? Shall we make a deal? If you won't take money, then at least I must buy you some wood and paint and varnish. And give you tea and cake whenever you come in. I'll carry on giving people the boxes – it's a great way of bringing customers into the shop."

Everyone was pleased with this, and Rosemary and Basil went away happy.

Hattie looked at Twister, who was sleeping peacefully. It was disappointing that Twister seemed to have nothing to do with this at all. And Hattie could already imagine what Mum would think. "Free gifts?" she'd say. "Typical Uncle Theo, that is. How he makes any money at all from that shop, I can't imagine."

Chapter Six

Rosemary and Basil got to work. They
brought boxes and boxes and boxes,
decorated with teddies, ducks and
flowers, as Hattie had suggested. Now,
instead of sneaking them out of their
pockets when they thought no one was
looking, Rosemary and Basil had a

special shelf of their own, where the Russian dolls used to be.

The boxes looked lovely. Hattie and Uncle Theo stood looking at them.

"You did well, there – solving the mystery, and making me sort things out with Rosemary and Basil," said Uncle Theo. "I want to give you a present –

yes, a reward! What would you like? One of the boxes, a special one? Or something else? Go on, choose! You can have anything you like."

"Thanks! *Can* I? Anything I like?"

"Anything you like," said Uncle Theo. "From the whole shop."

Hattie thought. But it didn't take her long to decide.

"I'd like Twister."

Uncle Theo started to speak, stopped, tried again. "Twister? You'd like…Twister?"

Hattie nodded.

"Yes, please."

"Then," said Uncle Theo, "you shall have Twister. As long as Mum says it's

all right." And he looked
down at the floor.

"Oh, she will!"
said Hattie. And
she bounded to
the window
to tell
Twister all
about it.

Twister stared,
blinked, then
went back to sleep.

As soon as Mum appeared in the
doorway, Hattie bounced up to her with
the exciting news. Mum looked
surprised – *very* surprised.

"Are you sure? Absolutely sure?" she
asked Uncle Theo.

"Yes, yes," said Uncle Theo, not quite looking at anyone. "I told Hattie she could have anything she wanted. So… well, no one's come to claim Twister, have they? If you want her, you'd better take her."

Mum started making arrangements. Back at home, she borrowed a cat carrier from Rita next door. Uncle Theo  gave them the cat food, cat biscuits and cat litter from the storeroom, and Twister's special cushion, too. Mum and Hattie went to the pet shop for a catnip mouse and a ball  with a bell in it.

Twister would have everything a cat could possibly want.

By next evening, Twister had moved in. Hattie moved a spare chair into her bedroom, and put Twister's cushion on it. Twister didn't look delighted with the new arrangement, but she soon began exploring.

Hattie drew a small, whiskered cat on the calendar in the kitchen, to mark the day as special.

She'd got what she wanted. So why didn't she feel happier?

The boxes looked lovely on the shelf, arranged there in clusters. But, by Friday week, Uncle Theo hadn't given away a single one. People looked at them, picked them up, admired them, asked about them. Several customers asked the price, but when Uncle Theo said that there *was* no price, they lost interest. Not one box had left the shop.

In fact, when Hattie looked around, there weren't many customers. No one browsing the shelves, no small child

 playing with the plastic cars, no one exclaiming over the panda with her baby.

It didn't feel right.

Ting! went the door, and she looked up hopefully as a man came in wearing a baby in a harness. But he only came as far as the doormat, already looking disappointed. The baby started to cry. *Ting!* went the door, as they left in a hurry.

Something just wasn't right.

Hattie cheered up when Rosemary and Basil called in to see how many more boxes were needed. They didn't look like Rosemary and Basil any more, because they had no need to wear their big coats with deep pockets. They looked just like everyone else, in a summer skirt and top (Rosemary) and baggy shorts and T-shirt (Basil). Hattie didn't even recognize them at first.

"Oh. Hello," said Uncle Theo, and reluctantly he led them to their shelf, which was just as they'd left it. All the boxes were still there. To Hattie's eye, they didn't look as bright and tempting as the first ones had. The teddies looked sad, the ducks seemed depressed, and the flowers drooped.

"Oh dear," said Rosemary, looking as if she might cry again. "See, it doesn't work this way."

"I think we'd better go back to what we did before," said Basil. "Come on, Rosemary. We've got shopping to do." And they left, not even waiting for tea and cake.

Hattie looked round at the empty shop. There wasn't a customer in sight. Outside, people were walking past the window without even glancing in. Just for something to do, Uncle Theo began rearranging the Roman gladiators.

"How's Twister?" he asked Hattie, as he always did.

Hattie shrugged. "She's okay." There was no more to say.

Mum came for her, and they went home. Every afternoon now, Hattie looked forward to seeing Twister. She hoped Twister would give her a special leg-twining welcome, the way she used to in the shop.

But Twister didn't do that any more. She hadn't done it since she'd moved to the house. She sat on the back doormat, looking bored. She glanced at Hattie, then looked away. Even her eyes weren't as bright or as green as before.

Hattie fetched Twister's furry mouse and dangled it; she found the ball-with-a-bell and rolled it. Twister wasn't at all interested, so Hattie stroked her instead.

"Oh, Twister! What's the matter?"

Not even the faintest purr. After a few

moments Twister got up and walked away. She jumped up to the window sill, and sat with her back to Hattie.

"She'll settle soon," said Mum. "Cats take a while to get used to a new home."

But Hattie had a bad feeling. All evening it nudged and nudged at her. She'd expected to be happy, with a cat of her own, but she wasn't.

She kept thinking of Uncle Theo's face when Mum carried Twister out of the shop. He looked just like that little boy, the one who hadn't been able to have the red tractor.

Hattie made up her mind.

On Saturday morning, Twister sniffed at her saucer of cat food, took one bored mouthful, then turned away.

"Mum," said Hattie. "Let's go and see Uncle Theo."

The shop was empty, in the way that had begun to seem normal. Uncle Theo was behind the till, doing the crossword, but very half-heartedly. He hadn't filled in many answers.

When he saw Hattie and Mum, he

gave a tired, sad sort of smile. Then his eyes widened as he saw who'd come with them.

Twister, in the cat carrier.

Twister sat inside, gazing around her
with bright green eyes. As soon as Mum
put the carrier down and opened the
front, she bounded out, and into her
window place.

At once, a family
passing by stopped to look,
smiling and laughing. Their
little boy tried to pat Twister through
the glass. Twister purred loudly, and
rubbed herself against the window.

"What's going on?" said Uncle Theo.

"We've brought her back," said Mum.

"To stay. She belongs here."

"But…Hattie?" Uncle Theo looked quite astonished. "She was your reward!"

"Yes," said Hattie, "but it wasn't right. Twister needs the shop. And the shop needs Twister."

Ting! went the door as the family came in, followed by three more customers.

"We like your shop cat!" they said, and, "Such bright green eyes!" and, "You'd think she owned the shop!"

"I've brought her cushion," said Mum. "Here, Twister!"

Twister gave a friendly chirrup. She jumped down, and twisted and twined herself round Uncle Theo's legs. Uncle Theo looked almost as if he might cry.

"Thank you, Hattie," he said. "Thank you."

Next, Twister went on a tour of inspection. She climbed up to the highest shelf to swipe her paw at an octopus mobile.

She checked
out the
Chinese
chequers.
She jumped up
into the rocking
horse's saddle.

"Hey, a real rocking horse!" said the
little boy's mum. "I've always wanted
one like that – could we find room for
it? Look at its dapples! Look at its lovely
brown eyes! *Could* we? Wouldn't you
like to ride on a real rocking horse,
Gavin?"

Gavin would, and fifteen minutes
later the horse had a SOLD tag tied to
its bridle. There was quite a queue by
now. Uncle Theo sold the octopus

mobile, a piggy bank and a kangaroo before he could pause for breath, or give proper attention to Twister. *Ting!* went the door, and *ting!* and *ting!* and *ting!* again, as customers going out with their parcels collided with people coming in. Among those were Rosemary and Basil, who – Hattie was delighted to see – were wearing their big coats again.

She sighed with happiness. This was more like it.

Then she noticed that the wooden boxes had gone from the shelf; the Russian dolls were back in their old place.

"Where are the boxes?" she asked Uncle Theo.

He paused, counting out change. "Oh

83

– I think you'll have to search for them. Or ask Twister."

The teenage girl who was next in the queue handed over a box. "I can't see a price on this!" she told him. "But it's *just* what I want! My little sister's in hospital, and she'd love this to put her hairslides and sparkly things in."

Uncle Theo smiled broadly as he looked at the green parrot on the box lid. "Have it. That's what it's meant for. For your sister to have in hospital. And I hope she gets better soon."

"No, but how much?" said the girl, not understanding.

"No charge. Nothing. It's hers," said Uncle Theo.

The girl thanked Uncle Theo and thanked him again, put the parrot box in her bag, then took it out again to look at, as if she couldn't quite believe it was real. Hattie noticed that Rosemary, standing nearby, looked pink and pleased.

Chapter Seven

A few days later, when Hattie arrived
from school, Twister gave a chirrup,
and twined herself round Hattie's legs.
Rosemary and Basil were there with
Uncle Theo; while Hattie was saying
hello to everyone, Twister walked off
purposefully towards the rocket-

launcher. She started dabbing with her paw at something half-hidden behind it.

Hattie looked. Wedged there, between a red drum and a xylophone, was a small painted box.

She reached, and picked it up.

It was by far the most beautiful of all the boxes so far. It was made of dark, dark wood, and on the lid was a picture of Twister. There she sat, in her most Twister-like way, paws neatly together. And her green eyes gazed, as wise and clever as the eyes of the *real* Twister.

"Thank you, Twister," Hattie whispered.

She carried the box very carefully to show Uncle Theo. "Look! Look what Twister's found! A box, the best one yet! The best one by *miles*!"

Uncle Theo and Rosemary and Basil all gathered round to look at it. Basil gave a secretive smile.

"Beautiful!" said Uncle Theo. "Twister to a T!"

"Have you looked inside?" said Rosemary.

Hattie opened the lid. The box was lined with red satin. Nestled there was a tiny black cat, carved of wood, with its tail high.

"A good-luck cat," said Uncle Theo. "And *this* box is for you. It must be – you're the one who found it!"

"They have a trick of finding their way to the right person," said Rosemary, beaming.

"It's the best present I could have!" said Hattie, and she took out the black cat and stood it in the palm of her hand.

And Twister, Uncle Theo's good-luck cat, jumped into the front window, turned round three times on her cushion, and settled down to sleep, with a small purry snore.

She was happy.

She was back in her proper place.

She was Shop Cat.

About the author

Linda Newbery loves to write. She also loves her four cats: Holly, Hazel, Finn and Fleur who keep her busy and who have inspired Cat Tales. Linda had her first novel published in 1988 and she's the author of many books for young readers. She has won the Silver Medal Nestlé Children's Book Prize and the Costa Children's Book Award.

Linda writes in a hut in her garden, usually with a cat or two for company.

Cat Tales

Curl up with Cat Tales from award-winning and enchanting storyteller, Linda Newbery.

The Cat with Two Names

Two of everything sounds perfect, but it soon leads to double the trouble for Cat...

ISBN 9780746096147

Rain Cat

Nobody believes that the mysterious cat can control the weather...until it starts to rain!

ISBN 9780746097281

Smoke Cat

Where do the shadowy cats in next door's
garden come from and why won't one
particular cat join them?

ISBN 9780746097298

Shop Cat

Strange things have started happening in the
toy shop since Twister came to stay...

ISBN 9780746097304

And coming soon...

The Cat who Wasn't There

Vincent is so lonely without his cat, Snow...
until a slim white cat appears in his garden.

ISBN 9780746097328

Ice Cat

Tom's cat is made of snow and ice, so of course
it can't come alive...or can it?

ISBN 9780746097311

For more fun and furry
animal stories, log on to
www.fiction.usborne.com